Put Beginning Readers on the Right Track with ALL ABOARD READING™

The All Aboard Reading series is especially for beginning readers. Written by noted authors and illustrated in full color, these are books that children really and truly *want* to read—books to excite their imagination, tickle their funny bone, expand their interests, and support their feelings. With three different reading levels, All Aboard Reading lets you choose which books are most appropriate for your children and their growing abilities.

Level 1—for Preschool through First Grade Children

Level 1 books have very few lines per page, very large type, easy words, lots of repetition, and pictures with visual "cues" to help children figure out the words on the page.

Level 2—for First Grade to Third Grade Children

Level 2 books are printed in slightly smaller type than Level 1 books. The stories are more complex, but there is still lots of repetition in the text and many pictures. The sentences are quite simple and are broken up into short lines to make reading easier.

Level 3—for Second Grade through Third Grade Children

Level 3 books have considerably longer texts, use harder words and more complicated sentences.

All Aboard for happy reading!

For sisters everywhere...
especially
Janine & Kristin
Jessica & Michelle.

And for my sister Diane,
who got the chicken pox.
And for Laura, who didn't.

Copyright © 1994 by Maryann Cocca-Leffler. All rights reserved. Published by Grosset & Dunlap, Inc., which is a member of The Putnam & Grosset Group, New York. ALL ABOARD READING is a trademark of The Putnam & Grosset Group. GROSSET & DUNLAP is a trademark of Grosset & Dunlap, Inc. Published simultaneously in Canada. Printed in the U.S.A.

Library of Congress Cataloging-in-Publication Data

Cocca-Leffler, Maryann
        What a pest! / by Maryann Cocca-Leffler.
            p.   cm. — (All aboard reading)
        Summary: Little sister Jessie is a nuisance at day camp, until a crisis threatens to ruin the talent show and she saves the day.
        [1. Sisters—Fiction. 2. Camps—Fiction. 3. Talent shows—Fiction.] I. Title. II. Series.
    PZ7.C638Wh   1994
    [E]—dc20   93-34126
                                                                                                     CIP
ISBN 0-448-40399-4 (GB)   A B C D E F G H I J   AC

ISBN 0-448-40393-5 (pbk.)   A B C D E F G H I J

ALL
ABOARD
READING™

Level 1
Preschool-Grade 1

WHAT A PEST!

By Maryann Cocca-Leffler

Grosset & Dunlap • New York

At last! Summer is here!
Now Meg comes over
every day.

My little sister Jessie
is always in the way.
What a pest!

She wants to play games
with us.

She wants to ride
her bike with us.

She wants to hear
our secrets.

She is even going
to day camp with us.
But Jessie is just a Guppy.
Meg and I are Sharks.

Guppies swim in the kiddy pool.

Sharks swim
in the big pool.

Guppies eat lunch inside.
Sharks eat lunch
at picnic tables.

After lunch,
Guppies take naps.

Sharks play cards or read.

Camp is great.
Jessie cannot bug us at all!

Soon there will be
a talent show.
Meg and I are going
to do a tap dance.
Tea for Two
is our song.
If we win,
we will split
a banana split
at Scoops.

Every day after camp,
Meg and I work
on our dance.
We put dimes
on our party shoes
to make loud taps.

We tap in the backyard.

We tap up in my room.

We tap in the living room.
Jessie is always around.

One morning
I hear tap tap
tapping.
I open the
bathroom door.
There is Jessie—
tap tapping away.
"Now it can be
Tea for Three!"
she says.
"No way!" I say.

I run into my parents' room.
"Why does she have to do
everything I do?" I ask.
My mom says,
"She loves you.
She wants to be
just like you."
But I am mad.

Now we only tap
at Meg's house.
Our costumes are great.
They look like teacups.

The talent show
is tomorrow.
I can almost taste
that **BIG** banana split!

The next morning
the phone rings.
It is Meg.
She has the chicken pox!

"Oh no!" I say.
"It is Tea for Two.
Not Tea for One!
I can't do it alone."

"I can take Meg's place,"
Jessie says.
"I can do all the steps."

Well...
that is true.

"Jessie, I will let you
dance with me.
But, from now on,
you can't always bug
Meg and me.
Is it a deal?"
Jessie thinks for a while.
"It's a deal."
Then we lock pinkies
on it.

On the way to camp,
we stop at Meg's house.
We get her costume.
"Good luck!" she calls
to us.

Before the show,
I am a little scared.
But Jessie is not scared
at all.

Then the music starts.
Jessie knows every step.
She is great.
I am great.
We are great.

We win first prize!

The next week,
we go to Scoops.
Meg is with us.
We split the banana split—
three ways.

And I don't mind at all!